My School's a Zoo!

By Stu Smith • Illustrated by David Catrow

HarperCollinsPublishers

Yesterday's trip to the zoo
left me feeling rather strange,
like my life was somehow different,
or just about to change.

My parents didn't look the same.
I watched them snort and drool.
My sister ate my homework.
I'm glad it's time for school.

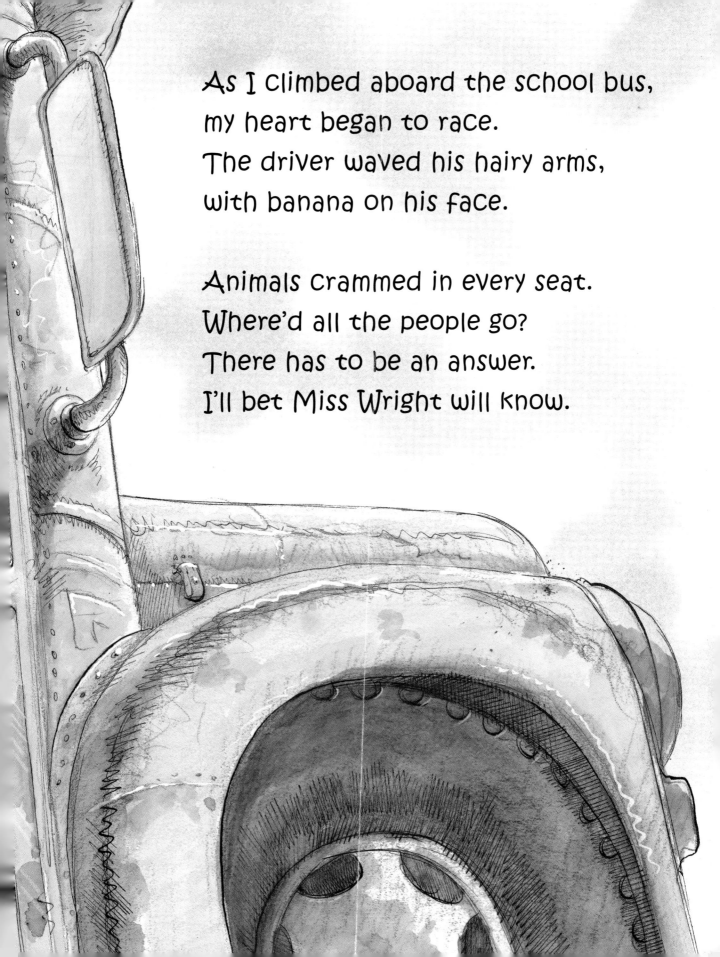

As I climbed aboard the school bus,
my heart began to race.
The driver waved his hairy arms,
with banana on his face.

Animals crammed in every seat.
Where'd all the people go?
There has to be an answer.
I'll bet Miss Wright will know.

I ran into my classroom,
but my teacher wasn't there.
I would have told the sub,
if she hadn't been a bear.

There were beehives in my desk,
and lizards at my feet.
A goat ate all my pencils.
There were needles on my seat.

By the time I got to art class,
there was nothing I could do.
There were pythons on the ceiling,
wreaking havoc with the glue.

Computer lab was crazy.
The mice were eating slugs.
The computers didn't work,
on account of all the bugs.

I tried to call for help,
but a yak was on the phone.
The principal was useless—
he was gnawing on a bone.

The librarian caught me hiding,
and she threw me quite a look.
As I glanced around the room,
I noticed worms in every book.

The lunchroom sure was crowded,
and the aides looked pretty mean.
The lions and the wildebeest
were causing quite a scene.

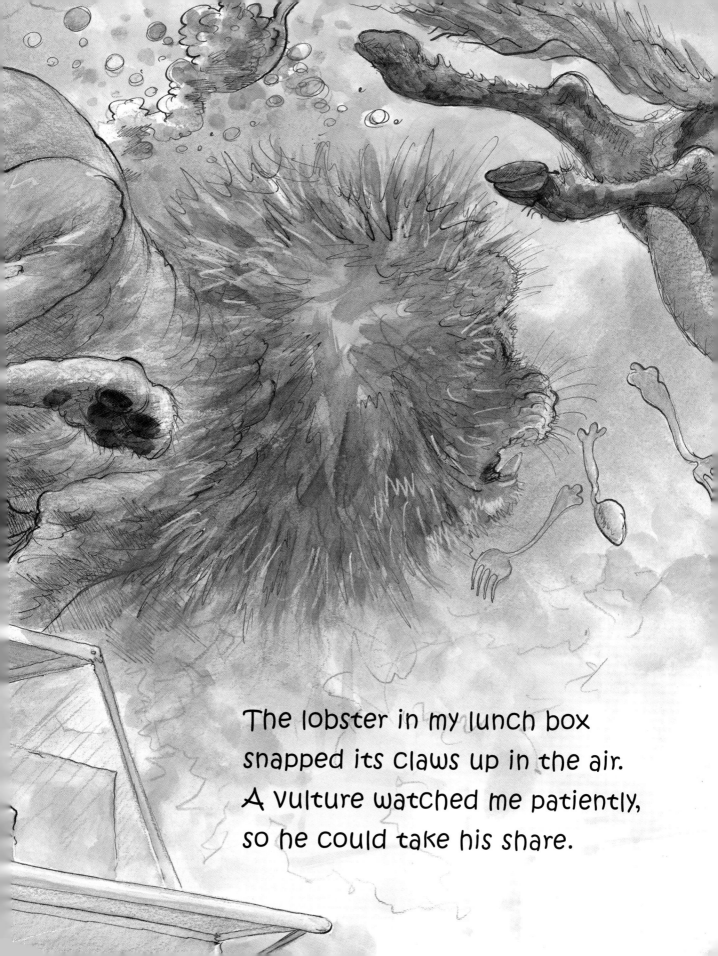

The lobster in my lunch box
snapped its claws up in the air.
A vulture watched me patiently,
so he could take his share.

The turtles on the playground
were spinning down the slide,
while hyenas laughed in chorus,
as a hippo took a ride.

Music class was noisy.
A penguin led our band.
The ostrich missed his cue,
and the monkey smashed his hand.

I was feeling kind of nauseous,
so I went to see the nurse,
but judging by her awful fangs,
I thought she'd make things worse.

There were starfish on my papers,
and a beaver cleaned the boards.
The seal clapped two erasers,
while a fox gave out awards.

The bus ride home was dreadful.
The skunks made quite a stink.
Did the zoo trip cause this mess?
I closed my eyes to think.

The next thing that I knew,
the driver tapped my hand.
Things seemed back to normal,
with my sister eating sand.

I sure hope that our next trip
to the dinosaur display
won't have the same effect
as the zoo trip did today.

But that could never happen,
the dinosaurs are gone.
At least I think they are.
Then again, I could be wrong . . .

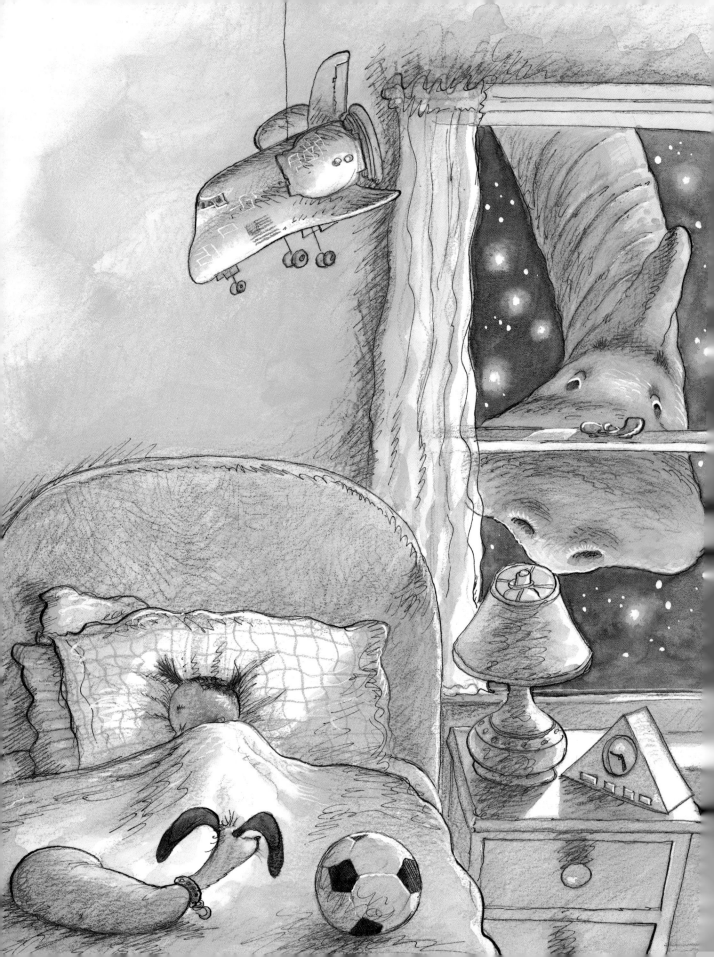

For Sue, Ryan, and Mackenzie
(Gracie and Koala too!)

—S.S.

To Judythe,
Every day is a birthday

—D.C.

My School's a Zoo
Text copyright © 2004 Stu Smith
Illustrations copyright © 2004 by David Catrow
Manufactured in China by South China Printing Company Ltd.
All rights reserved.
www.harperchildrens.com
Library of Congress Cataloging-in-Publication Data is available.
Typography by Elynn Cohen   1 2 3 4 5 6 7 8 9 10   ❖   First Edition